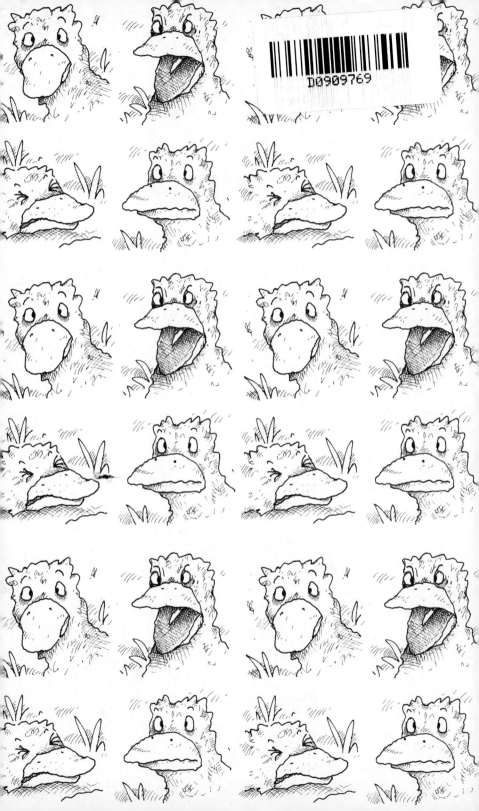
D0909769

Yucky Ducky

ALEX Kee

Yucky

Teh Funny, and Silly, Nice

J. M. DENT & SONS LTD London

Ducky

Fiendish, Sad and Nasty Tales

by David Henry Wilson

drawings by Jonathan Allen

Also by David Henry Wilson, published by Dent

How to Stop a Train with One Finger
Do Goldfish Play the Violin?
There's a Wolf in my Pudding
(*illustrated by Jonathan Allen*)

First published 1988
Text © David Henry Wilson 1988
Illustrations © Jonathan Allen 1988
All rights reserved

Typeset in Baskerville Roman
Printed and bound in Great Britain
by Butler & Tanner Ltd Frome and London
for J. M. Dent & Sons Ltd
91 Clapham High Street, London SW4 7TA

British Library Cataloguing in Publication Data
Wilson, David Henry,
Yucky ducky.
I. Title   II. Allen, Jonathan, 1957–
823'.914[J]

ISBN 0–460–07025–8

For Eric, Géraldine, young cousin Emma, Laurent, Antoine, and especially my goddaughter Corinne

Contents

Yucky Ducky

Once upon a time there was a Mother Duck who laid six eggs. Five of the eggs were extremely beautiful, and the sixth was extremely ugly.

'Look at our five extremely beautiful eggs!' cried Mother Duck.

'Look at your sixth extremely ugly egg!' cried Father Duck. 'Let's throw it in the river.'

But Mother Duck had once heard a story about an ugly duckling that had turned into a beautiful swan, and so she would not let her husband throw the sixth egg away. Instead she sat on it, together with the other eggs, week after week, as patiently as a picture of a statue of a stuffed duck in a glass case. Occasionally she would take a look at the eggs, and if anything five of them looked even more beautiful, and the sixth looked even more ugly. And then at last the eggshells began to break. One, two, three, four, five shells went pop, crackle, quack, and out came five extremely beautiful ducklings. And then the sixth egg went pop, crackle, ouch! Oh! Ah! And out came ... ugh! ... what a sight! It was presumably a duckling, but a 'more horrible, hideous, yuck of a duck it was impossible to imagine.

At first sight of him, Father Duck announced that he was going fishing, and was never seen again. As for the five extremely beautiful ducklings, they waddled round their ugly brother, beaking him with their bills and bumping him with their bottoms, quacking 'Yucky Ducky!' and making him cry. It wasn't, of course, a normal weepy wahwoo cry, but a harsh and air-splitting quaaaaaaark, which made even the local earwigs cover their ears with their wigs.

'Never mind, Yucky,' said Mother Duck. 'One day you'll turn into a beautiful swan, and make Mummy very proud of you.'

Then she took them all out on the river. The five beautiful ducklings swam smoothly and gracefully behind her, while the ugly duckling made all kinds of clumsy splashy movements and finally sank to the bottom of the river with a cry of 'He-e-e-lplug glug glug!' Fortunately, Mother Duck saw him sink. Quickly and quackly she dived to the bottom and pulled him up to the surface. He was covered with mud and hardly breathing. Mother Duck laid him on the river bank and gave him the quack of life, whereupon he opened his amazingly ugly, look-in-all-directions eyes and began to quaaaaaaark.

'Quaaaaaaark!' he cried. 'Quaaaaaaark, I can't even ... quaaaaaaark ... swim!'

'Mucky Yucky can't even swim!' jeered his extremely beautiful brothers and sisters.

'Never mind, darling,' said Mother Duck. 'One day you'll turn into a beautiful swan and swim better than all of us.'

Then she took her ducklings for a waddle through
the woods. The five beautiful ducklings waddled
steadily and proudly behind their mother, while the
ugly duckling kept falling over or bumping into trees.
Finally he got caught in a gorse bush and couldn't get
free.

'He-e-e-lp ouch ... oof ... ark ... quaaaaaaark!' he
cried.

'Yucky's stucky!' jeered his brothers and sisters.

Mother Duck pecked the thorny branches away from
the unlucky stucky Yucky, and he managed to stagger
clear before he tripped over the root of a tree, stumbled,
tumbled, and banged his beak on the bark.

'Quaaaaaaark!' he cried. 'I can't even ...
quaaaaaaark ... waddle!'

'Never mind, lovey,' said Mother Duck. 'One day you'll turn into a beautiful swan and waddle better than all of us.'

Then she took them for a toddle along a country road where there were no gorse bushes, no muddy water, no holes to fall down, no roots to trip over, and no trees to bump into. All there was, as it turned out, was a large lorry which had chosen exactly the same route as Mother Duck. And in less time than it takes to say 'Quack!' or 'Quaaaaaaark!' or 'I say, isn't that a rather large lorry coming towards us?' the lorry had run over one mother duck and five extremely beautiful ducklings who suddenly became five extremely flattened ducklings. And Yucky, who had tripped over his own feet and fallen at the side of the road, now found himself all alone in the world. At this moment some might have called him "Lucky Yucky", but he sat at the side of the road and quaaaaaaarked as loudly as if he had been run over himself. Even louder, in fact, since a run-over duckling probably wouldn't quaaaaaaark at all.

The lorry driver climbed out of his lorry, and when he saw the line of duck and ducklings all squashed in the road, he was a very sorry lorry driver. But there was nothing he could do. Then he heard Yucky quaaaaaaarking and went to have a look. One look was all he needed.

'Goodness gracious me!' he said (or words to that effect). 'Wot a 'orrible sight. You're an even worse mess than yer brothers an' sisters!'

There was clearly nothing he could do for Yucky either, and so he climbed into his lorry and drove away.

'Quaaaaaaark!' cried Yucky 'I can't even... quaaaaaaark ... get myself run over!'

He waited for a voice to tell him that one day he would turn into a beautiful swan and get himself run over better than all of them, but no voice spoke. And so he sat at the side of the road feeling very unrun-over, ugly and alone.

Now, although Yucky was extremely ugly he was not extremely stupid. Stupid, yes, but not *extremely* stupid. And he finally came up with what was really rather a clever thought. If he was one day going to turn into a beautiful swan, maybe he could find some swans now and ask them to look after him. He didn't actually know what swans looked like, or where they lived, but he did know that a live swan was more likely to help him than a dead duck.

The only clue Yucky had was the fact that swans were beautiful, and so as he waddle-totter-trip-fell along the road, he looked out for something beautiful. While he was looking, he happened to trip-fall into a ditch and, as he lay sprawled in the water, he found one of his eyes gazing at a very beautiful creature that was resting on a wild flower beside the ditch. It had red and gold wings with black spots, and although it was a lot smaller than himself, he thought it would be nice to be so beautiful.

'Excuse me,' he said, 'but are you a swan?'

'No, my deah,' said the creature. 'Ai'm a buttahflay. And why do you think Ai maight be a swan?'

'Because you're so beautiful,' said Yucky, 'and I know swans are beautiful.'

19

'Ai am beautiful, that's twue,' said the butterfly, 'but swans are gweat big things, whaile Ai'm extwemely delicate and fwagile. No, you poor ugly cweature: a buttahflay, thet's what Ai am.'

And so now Yucky knew that swans were great big things, and he waddle-toddled away into the forest to search for them.

Before long he saw a great big thing that was very beautiful indeed. It was standing beneath a tree and it had four legs, large eyes, and huge antlers on its head.

'Excuse me,' said Yucky, 'but are you a swan?'

'A swan?' bellowed the animal. 'Me? Mighty, massive, majestic me? No, you poor ugly little whatever-you-are, I'm a stag. King of the forest – though don't tell the lion I said so.'

'I know that swans are big and beautiful,' said Yucky, 'and you're big and beautiful, so I thought you were a swan.'

'Swans,' said the stag, 'may seem big and beautiful to you, but nothing, absolutely nothing, could be as big or as beautiful as I am. Besides, swans are birds. Whoever heard of a bird that could be compared with a stag? Whoever heard of *anything* that could be compared with a stag?'

And so now Yucky knew that swans were beautiful great big birds, and he stagger-stumbled further into the forest to see if he could find them.

Before long he saw a great big bird that was very beautiful indeed. It was perched on the branch of a tree, and it had huge wings, glittering eyes, and a curved beak.

'Excuse me,' said Yucky, 'but are you a swan?'

'You gotta be kiddin',' said the bird. 'A swan? Me? Do I look like a swan?'

'Well,' said Yucky, 'I was told swans are great big beautiful birds, and you're big and beautiful . . .'

'Ain't it de truth!' said the bird. 'I'm de biggest an' beautifullest boid in de forest, an' I could eat a swan for breakfast. I'd eat you, too, if you wasn't so unappetisin'. Eagle, dat's me. King o' de boids.'

'Quaaaaaaark!' cried Yucky. 'I shall never . . . quaaaaaaark . . . find the swans!'

'Aw quit quarkin',' snapped the eagle. 'It gets on my noives. Go an' jump in de river – dat's where de swans hang out.'

And so Yucky totter-tumbled away in search of the river. But he was now very tired. If he had been bumping into things and falling over before, he was now bumping-bumping and falling-falling twice as much. At last his right foot tripped over his left foot and he fell down beside a muddy pond. He didn't bother to get up again.

'Quaaaaaaark!' he cried.

'Aaaaaaark!' cried a voice next to his right ear.

'Quaaaaaaark!' said Yucky again, thinking it had been an echo.

'Aaaaaaark!' said the echo.

Yucky looked up and saw the ugliest creature he had ever seen (not counting Yucky himself, though he had not actually seen himself, since mirrors don't grow on trees). The creature was brown and squat, had long hind legs with webbed feet, short front legs, big eyes, and a wide mouth, and it was covered with warts.

'Crikey!' exclaimed Yucky. 'Aren't you ugly!'

'Croakey!' exclaimed the creature (which was a toad). 'I'm not as ugly as you!'

'You're uglier than me!' cried Yucky.

'Nothing could be uglier than you!' cried the toad.

'When I grow up,' said Yucky, 'I shall be a beautiful swan.'

'When I grow up,' said the toad, 'I shall be a hand-some prince.'

'Why don't you both grow up,' said a passing rat, 'and be yourselves.'

'Don't take any notice of him,' said the toad. 'He's just a dirty rat.'

Then the toad told Yucky that he was searching for a palace, where he would live happily ever after. Yucky said that if he ever bumped into a palace he would let the toad know. Then Yucky told the toad that he was searching for a river, where all his troubles would be over.

'You're lucky,' said the toad. 'Rivers are easy to find.'

'Nothing's easy for me to find,' said Yucky. 'Sometimes I can't even find my own feet.'

Yucky and the toad became good friends, and they decided to stay together until they became a swan and a prince. They waited a long time. The only change that Yucky saw in the toad was that he seemed to get smaller and uglier. The toad, on the other hand, thought Yucky was growing bigger and uglier. And Yucky himself certainly felt that he was bigger. He also found out that he could not only swim a few yards in the pond but even fly a few yards through the air – before crashing in a crumpled heap on the earth. All this seemed to be a sign that he had now grown up, and if he had grown up, then he must surely have turned into a swan.

'Well,' he said to the toad, 'that's it.'

'That's what?' asked the toad.

'I'm a swan,' said Yucky.

'You're kidding,' said the toad.

'No, I'm not,' said Yucky. 'I'm swanning.'

'If you're a swan,' said the toad, 'then I'm a handsome prince.'

'Quackle quackle quackle!' cackled Yucky. 'I've never seen a handsome prince as ugly as you!'

'Uckle uckle uckle!' chuckled the toad. 'You're so ugly, you're more like a swine than a swan!'

'Well, you're not a handsome prince,' said Yucky.

'I know,' said the toad. 'And you're not a swan.'

But although the toad knew he was not a handsome prince, Yucky was still sure he was a swan, and so he decided to set out for the river to find his fellow swans. It so happened that the toad had found out where the river was.

'All you have to do,' he said, 'is follow the track straight over that hill. That is, if you *can* ever go straight over anything.'

'What are *you* going to do?' asked Yucky.

'I'm going to look for the road to the palace,' said the toad.

And so the two of them said goodbye to each other and went their separate ways.

'Hope you find the right roadie, Toadie!' called Yucky.

'Stay on the trackie, Quackie!' shouted the toad.

Yucky waddled (and fell) and flew (and fell) along the track which led over the hill and finally down to the river. It was a clear, calm, sunny day and, as he stood on the river bank where he had spent so many miserable days in the past, he felt that he had come home. And when, out in the middle of the river, he caught sight of two graceful, long-necked, elegant white birds gliding through the water, he just knew that these were swans and he was one of them.

'Hullo, there!' he cried, and dived with a great sploshy splash into the water.

The swans took no notice, but Yucky waggled his feet and flapped his wings and managed to crash-whoosh his way towards them.

'Hullo, there!' he cried again. 'Wait for me!'

'Are you speaking to us?' asked the male swan.

'Yes!' puffed Yucky. 'You're swans, aren't you?'

'Of course we're swans,' said the female swan.

'Great!' said Yucky. 'Then we can all be swans to-gether.'

'We don't want riff-raff like that around here,' said the female swan. 'Marcel, chase him off.'

Marcel, the male swan, immediately raced towards Yucky and gave him a fearful peck on the bottom.

'Quouch!' cried Yucky.

'Quack off!' cried Marcel.

'But I'm not an ugly duckling any more!' howled Yucky. 'I'm a swan like you!'

'Don't be insulting!' said Marcel, and added a second peck to the first.

Yucky didn't wait for a third peck. Quaaaaaaarking with pain and fear, he whoosh-crashed his way back towards the river bank, while Marcel and his wife sailed serenely away down the river, discussing the lowered tone of the neighbourhood.

Yucky stood on the river bank and sadly watched them go. Why hadn't they welcomed him? Why had they called him riff-raff? Why had they pecked his bottom?

Yucky's head dropped with the weight of his disappointment, and he found himself gazing down into the calm water. And the reflection that he saw there gave him the answer to all his questions. He had been right: he had grown up. And now, instead of being an extremely ugly duckling, he had turned into an extremely ugly duck.

The Arly Bard

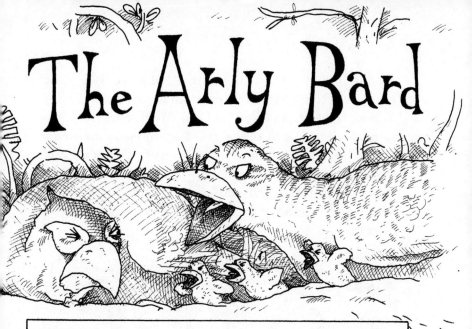

'Kark kark!' squawked Phyllis the Pheasant. 'Kark kark, wake arp!'

'Aw shurrup! Keep quiet! Go to sleep!' came a chorus of complaining bird voices.

'Marmy, Marmy, we're hungry, hungry!' came a chorus of baby squawks.

'What a larvely marning!' shrilled Phyllis. 'Carme on, Freddy, time to wake arp!'

'Ugh, ah, ugh!' groaned her husband. 'I'm still asleep. Leave us alone!'

'Let's be arp before the lark, shall we?'

'You can be up before the lark. I've still got some sleeping to do.'

'Marmy, Marmy, we're hungry, hungry!'

'Freddy, our babies are starving! Wake arp! Now! Kark kark!'

'Caw, what a row!' said a crow.

'She's ravin'!' said a raven.

'Quiet! Shurrup! Put a gag on her!' came the chorus.

Meanwhile, down in the hunting lodge, tucked away among the trees, Mr and Mrs Smith woke up and smiled at one another. The sun had just risen, and the birds were singing. It was the perfect beginning to their new life in their new home. Far away from the noise and fumes of the traffic, the rushing and pushing of the crowds, the rattle and clatter of machines, here they had found perfect peace in the harmonious midst of Nature.

'Oh, John,' said Mrs Smith, 'listen to the birds. It's the dawn chorus.'

'Beautiful,' said Mr Smith. 'All those happy birds, welcoming the new day with their joyful melodies.'

'Apart from that awful *kark kark* noise,' said Mrs Smith. 'I wonder what that can be.'

'It sounds like someone strangling a cat!' said Mr Smith.

'How horrible!' said Mrs Smith.

'But the birds are beautiful,' said Mr Smith.

'Gorgeous,' said Mrs Smith.

'Kark kark!' said Phyllis. 'Freddy, *will* you get arp?'

'We want breakfast! We want breakfast!' wailed the babies.

'Kark kark, the arly bard cartches the warm!' screeched Phyllis.

'I'll be quite happy with a beakful of berries,' said Freddy.

'We want worms! We want worms!' squealed the babies.

'And warms you shall harve!' blared Phyllis. 'Arp, Freddy! Arp! Arp!'

'Even the worms'll be asleep at this hour!' groaned Freddy.

'Arp! Arp!'

'Coo coo cool it!' said a dove.

'She's quackers!' said a duck.

'Will you stop that noise! Put some glue in her beak! Shut her up!' came the chorus.

From all round the forest came voices of birdy protest. A blackbird said it was still pitch dark in his part of the wood (though he had his head under his wing at the time), and the lark – who was always the first to rise – called out that it was far too unpleasant for a pheasant, since it was much too dark for a lark. The birds all agreed that Phyllis was making a nuisance of herself, and they said so in their loudest voices.

'I think,' said Mrs Smith, 'they must be singing extra loud just for us, John, to welcome us to the wood.'

'They're certainly singing lovesongs,' said Mr Smith.

'How do you know?' asked Mrs Smith, with a little giggle.

'Only lovesongs could sound as sweet as that,' said Mr Smith.

'Kark kark!' said Phyllis. 'Arp, Freddy! Arp, arp!'

'I don't think that's a lovesong,' said Mrs Smith.

'No,' said Mr Smith, 'that's an awful row.'

'We want worms, we want worms!' squealed the baby pheasants.

'I want sleep!' moaned the Daddy pheasant.

'Arp arp arp!' arped the Mummy pheasant.

'She's batty!' said a bat.

'Queep quiet!' wailed a quail.

'Kark kark, the arly bard cartches the warm!' trumpeted Phyllis.

'We shall have to do something about that awful noise,' said Mrs Smith. 'It's spoiling the whole dawn chorus.'

'I've got a feeling,' said Mr Smith, 'that that's a bird as well. Let's look it up.'

Mr Smith got out of bed, turned on the light, and went to the bookshelf in the living room. He took out his *Big Encyclopaedia of Birds*, went back into the bedroom, and climbed into bed. Together, he and Mrs Smith looked through the section on bird calls. There was *alleyoop* for the crane, *billycoo* for the lovebird, *charge* for the bullfinch, *dingdong* for the bellbird, *'eavenly* for the bird of paradise, *fedup* for the grouse, *glug* for the swallow, *hmmmmmm* for the humming bird, *inigo* for the diver, *jeery* for the mocking-bird and . . . *kark*.

'It's a pheasant!' said Mr Smith.

'A pheasant?' said Mrs Smith.

'A pheasant!' said Mr Smith.

'Kark!' said Phyllis. 'I can see I sharl harve to cartch the warms myself if the darlings are to harve thar breakfast.'

'What a twit!' twittered a tit.

'And twit to you, too!' howled an owl.

'We'd like some hush!' thrilled a thrush.

'Sleep's what we'd like!' shrieked a shrike.

'Are you thinking what I'm thinking?' Mr Smith asked Mrs Smith.

'I think so,' said Mrs Smith. 'Lunch?'

'Clever girl!' said Mr Smith. 'Let's catch lunch, and then have breakfast.'

They dressed very quickly, listening all the time for signs that the pheasant was still there.

'Kark!' said Phyllis.

It was.

'Where are our worms? We want our worms!' squealed the babies.

'It's your larst charnce, Freddy,' bugled Phyllis. 'Are you getting arp or aren't you?'

'I aren't,' said Freddy.

'Then I'm going,' said Phyllis.

'Good,' said Freddy.

'And when I carme bark,' said Phyllis, 'I shall feed our darlings, and then we sharl arl go to my marther's and nevar retarn.'

'Yippee!' said Freddy.

'Quite right!' said a kite.

'Turn her loose!' said a goose.

'Let her go!' said a crow.

By now Mr and Mrs Smith were dressed. Mr Smith had taken his special hunting gun out of its case and had loaded it with special pellets. Mrs Smith had taken her special cooking pot from its shelf and had loaded it with special spices. The two of them now went to the door of the house, opened it, and stepped out into the dim light of dawn.

'It's no good,' said Mrs Smith. 'We'll never see it amongst all those trees and leaves and branches.'

At that precise moment, Phyllis the Pheasant whirred her wings and took off to hunt for worms, with a final kark and a cry of:

'The arly bard cartches the . . .'

BANG BANG BANG!

The arly bard caught a good deal more than she'd expected to catch . . .

The baby pheasants didn't get their breakfast until the sun had finished rising and their father had finished sleeping. Phyllis never had any breakfast at all. But Mr and Mrs Smith had a wonderful lunch.

The Leopard that Wouldn't Eat Meat

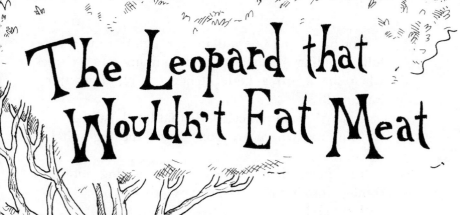

Lena the Leopard was very short-sighted. She was famous for bowing to deer and biting lions, for saying hello to tree trunks and climbing up elephants, and for her fierce and never-ending battles with thorn bushes. When she was out hunting, her only chance of success lay in finding animals that were old, lame, blind, or just plain stupid. Fortunately, there were enough of these to keep her from starving.

One day, Lena was walking through the forest, carefully avoiding the shadows and bumping into the trees, when she heard a high-pitched cry of, 'I want my mummy!'

'Aha!' she said to herself. 'Is that lunch calling?'

'Mummy, where are you?' cried the high-pitched voice.

'I'm here, dear!' called Lena, putting motherly comfort into her tone. 'Where exactly are you?'

'I'm here!'

'Where's here?'

'Under this bush.'

By following the sound of the voice, Lena – thinking cheerful thoughts about easy meat – slowly made her way towards its owner.

'Over here, Mummy! Look, I'm over here! This way ... Oops ... you're not my mummy!'

Lunch saw the leopard long before the leopard saw lunch, and Lena's thoughts of easy meat gave way to thoughts of no meat at all.

'Your mummy sent me to look after you,' she called out quickly, 'because she loves you so much, and so do I.'

'Where *is* my mummy?' asked the high-pitched voice.

'She's gone to see your daddy,' replied Lena.

'Where is my daddy?' asked the voice.

'Waiting for your mummy,' replied Lena.

In front of her she could see a blurred, four-legged shape that seemed to have lunch written all over it. But just as she was about to pounce, she saw that there was something else all over the four-legged shape: spots. Big brown spots, just like her own.

'Oh!' said Lena. 'You've got spots.'

'So have you,' said Lunch.

'What a nuisance!' said Lena.

'Mine aren't,' said Lunch. 'Mine are very nice.'

But they were a nuisance for Lena because of a special rule in the forest: leopards are allowed to eat anything except other leopards. And if the blurred four-legged shape had spots, it must be a leopard.

'There goes lunch!' said Lena.

'Where?' asked Lena's ex-lunch.

Now this gave Lena an idea. A cub wouldn't be any good at hunting, but it would be very useful for seeing, and if this cub could just point Lena in the right direction, she might be able to catch lunch for both of them. The cub, whose name was Jerry – a strange name, since most leopards are called Larry or Luke or Lancelot – also thought it was a good idea. And so off they went together in search of a good meal.

It should have been the perfect arrangement. But what is a good meal? With Jerry's help, Lena caught a juicy young deer, but to her amazement Jerry refused to take a single bite.

'But it's lovely fresh meat!' cried Lena.

'I know,' said Jerry, 'but I don't like meat.'

'Nonsense!' cried Lena. 'Spiders eat flies, monkeys eat bananas, and leopards eat meat. That's the law, so put this between your teeth and chew it.'

So saying, she presented Jerry with a tender slice straight from the deer's bottom. That may not sound very yum-yum to you, but a slice of deer's bottom to a leopard is like a slice of chocolate fudge cake to a human.

Jerry chewed it, and chewed it, and chewed it . . .

'Well, how does it taste?' asked Lena.

'Yuck!' said Jerry, and spat it out on the ground.

Lena didn't see the spitting, but she heard the yucking. What could be the matter with this strange cub? Was he too young to know a good thing when he chewed it? Had he lost his teeth? Had someone invented a new diet for cubs?

Lena had never had any cubs of her own. She'd looked for a mate, but being so short-sighted, she'd never found one. Occasionally male leopards had approached her, but male leopards soon get tired of being asked where they are. And they don't like leopardesses that walk straight past them and give a loving kiss to an anthill.

With no cubs of her own, then, Lena didn't quite know what to expect.

'What do you normally eat?' she asked.

'Leaves,' said Jerry.

'You must be joking,' said Lena. 'Leaves aren't food!'

'Yes, they are,' said Jerry.

'Leaves are leaves,' said Lena. 'Meat is food.'

'Meat is yuck,' said Jerry. 'Leaves are food.'

'In that case,' said Lena, 'you can get your own lunch.'

'In that case,' said Jerry, 'so can you.'

Since Lena already had her lunch, she shrugged her shoulders and carried on munching her deer. If Jerry was going to be stupid and stubborn, then let him. He'd soon come crawling when he wanted a proper meal.

But Lena was to find that being a mother leopard was not so simple. For one thing, Jerry turned out to be a very disobedient cub. He said that if she wouldn't help him catch leaves, then he wouldn't help her catch meat. Lena therefore found herself compelled to go leaf-hunting. With Jerry's directions, she climbed the right tree, walked along the right branch, bit off the right leaves, and dropped them down in the right place. Unfortunately, Jerry then stopped giving her directions and she took a wrong step and fell off the branch. As a result of this painful experience she refused to do any more leaf-hunting, and so Jerry refused to do any more meat-hunting, and that left Lena feeling very hungry.

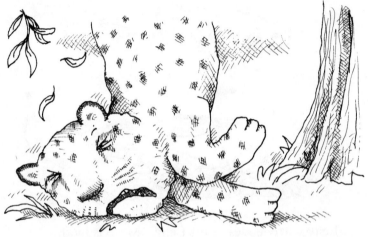

But not only was Lena hungry and Jerry disobedient. Another problem began to worry the mother leopard. One night, when Jerry happened to fall asleep very close to her, she noticed that he smelled rather strange.

'Phew!' she said. 'Body odour!'

The cub obviously needed a good wash, but when she began to lick him, she realized that he was quite amazingly thin. His legs were just like sticks, and his bones stuck out through his skin like lumps of rock through grass.

'This is what comes of eating leaves!' she growled.

Eating leaves was as unhealthy as not eating meat, and if she didn't do something soon, then she and Jerry would clearly starve to death.

In the whole of the forest there was only one creature who could find a cure for this strange disease. Doctor Duck, the famous quack doctor, had an answer to every question, a medicine for every illness, and (if necessary) an excuse for every failure.

It took Lena and Jerry three days to find the doctor. Lena knew the way but couldn't see it, and Jerry could see the way but didn't know it. And directions like "Turn left at the jacaranda tree" aren't much help if there are jacaranda trees all around you. (And in any case, do *you* know what a jacaranda tree looks like?) But at last they arrived, and Lena told Doctor Duck the whole story from start to finish.

Doctor Duck listened in silence, apart from an occasional "quack", "quumbs" or "quikey", and when Lena had finished, he pulled out a special instrument called a dabblescope. With this he listened to Jerry's

heartbeat, tested his blood pressure, took his temperature, measured his neck, chest, and inside leg, checked his eyesight, hearing and tonsils, looked up his nose, down his throat, and through his legs, tapped his knee, twitched his tail, tweaked his ears, and finally tickled his tummy.

'Well, Doctor?' asked Lena. 'Can you cure him?'

'No, I quan't,' quacked the doctor, 'bequause I quan't find any quomplaint, quondition or handiquap. Jerry is quompletely normal.'

'Normal!' cried Lena. 'Who's ever heard of a leopard that wouldn't eat meat? That's not normal!'

'Quite quorrect,' said the doctor. 'It would be a queer quondition for a leopard. But its quite typiqual for a giraffe.'

And that, of course, explained everything. Giraffes are thin, giraffes eat leaves and not meat, and giraffes are called Jerry. And since Jerry at this moment was standing right next to Lena, he was able to solve two more of her problems straight away. No mother leopard likes to be disobeyed by her cub, and no mother leopard can do without her meat. And there is no rule in the forest that says a leopard can't eat a giraffe.

The Elephant that Forgot

Elephants have marvellous memories. If you give an elephant a currant bun, and ten years later you offer him another currant bun, he'll say: 'Fancy seeing you again!' And 'What took you so long?' And 'If I have to wait another ten years, I'll finish up the size of a dormouse.'

Some elephants have such good memories that they can even remember things that *didn't* happen. These things are called elefantasies. But most elephants that you meet in the street or the circus or the zoo (or the jungle, if you happen to be going that way) will stick to the elefacts.

There was, however one young elephant who simply had no memory at all for elefacts or even elefiction. Elvis was his name, and forgetful was his nature. He couldn't remember anything from one moment to the next. If someone asked him whether he'd like a currant bun, he'd say: 'What's a currant bun?' And when he'd eaten the currant bun, he'd say: 'What happened to that currant bun?' And when someone told him: 'You've eaten it, Elvis,' he'd say: 'Eaten what?' Or, 'Who's Elvis?'

Elvis's parents grew rather tired of Elvis's forget-fulness, because it was no elefun at all having to tell him over and over again who they were, who he was, what he'd done, where he'd been etc. Conversation with Elvis was like doing the long jump – to take one step forwards you had to take twenty steps backwards. Though if Elvis *had* been doing the long jump, he'd have only taken one step backwards and would then have for-gotten where he was going.

In the end, his parents decided to send him to a special elephant mind-doctor, called an elephanalyst, whose name was Dr Shrink Think Trunk (he came from the East). He was said to be very clever, and had once cured a mule of mulancholy, a parrot of parronoia, and a hippo of hippochondria. If anyone could cure Elvis's forgetfulness, he could.

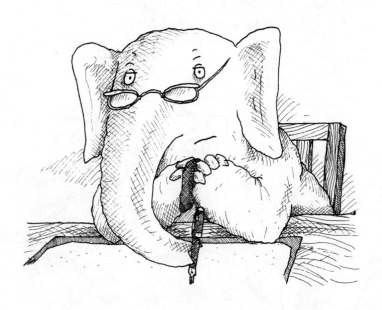

'Now then, Elvis,' said the doctor, 'what's the matter with you?'

'I can't remember,' said Elvis.

'You must have a bad memory,' said the doctor.

'Yes,' said Elvis.

'If you can't remember what's wrong with you, how am I supposed to cure you?'

'I don't know,' said Elvis.

'Nor do I,' said the doctor.

And so away went Elvis.

'How did you get on with the doctor?' asked Elvis's mother.

'What doctor?' asked Elvis.

Then Elvis's mother told Elvis's father to go with Elvis and explain everything to the doctor.

'I see,' said the doctor. 'Now then, Elvis, how long has this been going on?'

'How long has what been going on?' asked Elvis.

'Your loss of memory,' said the doctor.

'What loss of memory?' asked Elvis.

'This is a very difficult case,' said the doctor.

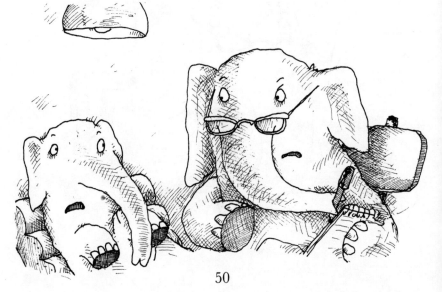

He then consulted his *Big Encyclopedia of Elefaults*, and
read out what it said under 'Loss of Memory':

"If an elephant has lost his memory, it is because he
cannot remember anything. The cure is to stop him
from forgetting."

'Well, that's clear enough,' said the doctor. 'Now
we're getting somewhere. All we have to do is stop you
from forgetting.'

'Forgetting what?' asked Elvis.

'Whatever you want to remember,' said the doctor.

'How are you going to stop him from forgetting?'
asked Elvis's father.

'I don't know,' said the doctor. 'That's *his* problem.'

Elvis's father thought it ought to be the doctor's
problem, but the doctor said he already had enough
problems without worrying about Elvis's. Elvis's father
said that was a pretty strange way of curing Elvis's
illness, and the doctor said that was fair enough because
Elvis's illness itself was pretty strange. Then Elvis's
father threatened to report the doctor to the Association
of Elephysicians, and the doctor remembered that he'd
already been reported twice and was in danger of being
disqualified. So he took down his *Big Encyclopedia of
Elephantidotes*, and read out what it said under 'Cures
for Loss of Memory':

"In order to remember not to forget something," it said, "tie a knot in your trunk."

'There you are,' said the doctor. 'Your troubles are over. Tie a knot in your trunk, and you can forget you ever lost your memory.'

So away went Elvis and his father and Elvis immediately tied a knot in his trunk to remind him that when he wanted to remember something, he must tie a knot in his trunk. Unfortunately, he couldn't remember what he'd tied the knot for, and so he tied another knot to remind him to ask his father why he'd tied the first knot. But with two knots in his trunk, he couldn't breathe, and so had to be rushed to the doctor's to get himself untied. (This was a different doctor, of course, who specialised in untying elephant knots, and was called an elephuntier.)

'What on earth did you tie those knots for?' asked the doctor, when he'd untangled Elvis's trunk.

'What knots?' asked Elvis.

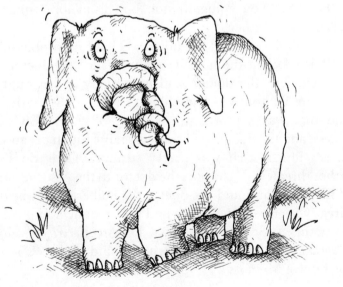

Elvis's mother was furious and she took him straight back to Dr Shrink Think Trunk herself. Then she trumpeted in the doctor's ear precisely what she thought of him. Not only, she said, had his method failed to cure her son's bad memory, but it had very nearly suffocated him to death.

'Well,' mumbled the doctor, 'that's one way of curing a bad memory.'

But as he was rather frightened of Elvis's mother, he looked around for another cure and came upon a book called *Elephamnesia* which he'd forgotten about before. He looked at the list of contents, checked the index, flicked through the footnotes, chased through the chapters, perused the paragraphs, and finally read out:

"In order not to forget to remember something, write it down."

'There you are,' he said. 'Your troubles are over. Write it down, and you'll remember happily ever after.'

So away went Elvis and his mother.

'Now then, Elvis,' said his mother, 'write down: "I must write down whatever I want to remember." '

'I can't,' said Elvis.

'Why not?' asked his mother.

'I can't write,' said Elvis.

'You great elefool!' said his mother. 'Why didn't you say so?'

'I forgot,' said Elvis.

And so back they went to the doctor who, when he saw them, screamed and banged his head three times against the wall.

'No more!' he cried. 'No more! I can't stand it!'

'Can't stand what?' asked Elvis.

Elvis's mother explained to the doctor that Elvis couldn't write, and so he'd have to find another cure. The doctor explained to her that there weren't any other cures, that he'd tried everything he knew, that Elvis was a hopeless case, and if Elvis's mother didn't take Elvis away very soon, then he – the doctor – would ask for himself to be taken away and treated for an acute attack of elephobia.

But Elvis's mother still wouldn't give up. If Dr Shrink Think Trunk couldn't cure her son, then she wanted to know who could. And so the doctor remembered a colleague of his in Tuskany, who was said to be the world's leading pachydermatologist (which means expert in elephant illnesses). He put through a long distance call (that's right, a trunk call) to this expert, who came up with a very clever idea:

'All you have to do,' reported the doctor, 'is ask other elephants to remind you. If, for instance, you forget who you are, then your parents can tell you. And if you forget what you have to do, then they'll tell you that, too. And if you forget where you've been, just ask. Never be afraid to ask. Ah, the simple solutions are always the best. Goodbye, goodbye, and please don't come back.'

So away went Elvis and his mother, and they told Elvis's father and all the other elephants about the new cure. And when Elvis forgot what the new cure was, his parents explained it to him, and when Elvis forgot who *he* was . . .

'Wait a minute,' said Elvis's mother. 'Isn't this what we were doing before?'

'Yes, it is,' said Elvis's father. 'And that's why we sent him to the doctor in the first place. Isn't it, Elvis?'

'What doctor?' said Elvis.

Elvis was right back where he'd started. Clearly there was no point in trying the doctor again, and the only way of dealing with Elvis's forgetfulness seemed to be to forget it. And then one day something very strange happened.

A little girl gave Elvis a currant bun, which he whiffled up with his trunk before swallowing it in a single gulp.

'Where's the currant bun gone?' he asked.

'You've eaten it,' said the little girl.

'Eaten what?' asked Elvis.

'The currant bun,' said the little girl.

'What currant bun?' asked Elvis.

Nothing very strange in that conversation, you might think. But then the little girl gave Elvis another currant bun. And when he'd eaten and forgotten that, she gave him a cream bun. And then a doughnut and a rock cake and a sponge cake and a chocolate gateau and a birthday cake and a wedding cake and a bag of peppermints and a packet of liquorice-all-sorts ... etc. etc. It was a real elefeast, and Elvis enjoyed every mouthful.

But that night, Elvis had a terrible tummy ache. It was the tummiest tummy and the achiest ache imaginable. It was a bellyphant of a tummy ache.

'Elephoh!' he cried. 'Elephouch! Elephah! Elephow!'

His parents at once sent for the elephuntier, because they thought Elvis might have tied a knot in his tummy.

'What,' the doctor asked Elvis, 'have you been eating?'

And it was then that the miracle happened.

'A currant bun,' gasped Elvis. 'And then another currant bun. And then a cream bun and a doughnut and a rock cake and a sponge cake and a chocolate gateau and . . .'

Elvis remembered every single thing that he'd eaten. He even remembered them in the order in which he'd eaten them.

That night he was horribly, disgustingly sick, and when he'd recovered from his sickness, his memory was cured as well, and he remembered happily ever after. You may think that it was a rather strange cure. But if you had eaten a currant bun, then another currant bun, then a cream bun, a doughnut, a rock cake, a sponge cake, a chocolate gateau, a birthday cake, a wedding cake, a bag of peppermints and a packet of liquorice-all-sorts, would you have forgotten?

Wolves 11 Rabbits 0

Hi there. Wolfie's the name. Mine, that is, not yours. (Unless yours happens to be Wolfie, too.) I'm the famous Wolfie that got unfairly and rather fatally killed by Red Riding Hood's grandma. You remember the story? Well, if you don't, too bad, because I'm not going to tell it to you. I've told that story so many times, I'm beginning to believe it's true.

No, this is a football story. We forest animals are crazy about football. Find a clearing, and you'll find two teams kicking a coconut. And what teams we've produced! Who hasn't heard of Monkeyster United, Assenal, Leoparpool, Toadenham Hotspawn? But the greatest team of all was without doubt The Wolves. And the greatest day of the greatest team was without doubt the day when we won the Forest Animals (F.A.) Cup. Modesty forbids me to mention that I was the captain. Well, I suppose I could mention it. I was the captain.

What a day that was! Of course, the F.A. Cup was the biggest competition in the forest. Maybe it still is. After Red Riding Hood's granny put four bullets in me, I kind of lost interest in football. In fact, I kind of lost interest in everything. But back in the good old pre-granny days, I just lived for football. And the proudest day of my life was when I led the team to victory in the F.A. Cup.

Forest football rules were the same as ordinary football rules except for one additional law: any player caught eating a member of the other side was automatically sent off. In the days when the good old days were not so good, there were a lot of sendings-off. There was one famous occasion during the grim winter of '78 when a third-round match between ourselves and the ducks ended with only the referee on the field. The match was abandoned as a draw, and the ducks never showed up for the replay.

Anyway I was telling you about the year we won the cup. And in particular, I want to tell you about the Cup Final. And particularly in particular, I want to tell you about the brilliant strategy that won us the cup. Under my captaincy, incidentally. Did I mention that I was captain?

We were due to play the rabbits, and we all knew we were in for a tough match. The rabbits had already won the cup two years running – and I mean running. Their main advantage was sheer speed. They were so fast that it always looked as if there were fifty of them on the field. Some of us reckoned there *were* fifty of them on the field. There might only have been eleven at the start, but you know how quick rabbits are at multiplying. Anyway, they were hot favourites to win, and we were the underdogs – or underwolves – or whatever you'd like to call us. Team morale was very low.

'We haven't got a chance,' moaned Wilfie, our goal-keeper. 'Look what they did to us last year.'

'What did they do to us last year?' I asked, pretending that it had slipped my memory.

'They beat us 47–0,' he groaned.

'Maybe you had an off day,' I suggested.

'Wilfie was the only one of us who touched the ball,' said Willy, our striker. 'Apart from me kicking off.'

'And then I was only picking it out of the back of the net,' said Wilfie.

'But that was *last* year,' I said, trying to lift their spirits.

'What's different this year?' asked our left wing.

'You've got me as captain,' I said.

'And what difference is that going to make?' asked our right wing.

Well, I couldn't really tell him. You don't expect that sort of question out of the blue.

I did what I could to encourage the team, but by the end of that training session, they'd convinced themselves that they'd be lucky to lose 50–0.

'Think positive,' I said. 'If we do as well as last year, it'll only be 47–0.'

But they wouldn't listen.

When I got home, my wife noticed that I wasn't my usual cheerful self.

'What's the matter with you?' she asked. 'You look as if you've just been invited to the woodcutters' ball.'

My wife was very sensitive to my feelings. I told her the problem.

'Ugh, ugh,' she said. 'You and your football. It's only a game, isn't it?'

My wife didn't know very much about football.

'A game?' I said. 'A GAME? It's the F.A. Cup Final!'

'Isn't that a game?' she asked.

Patiently, I explained to her just what the F.A. Cup Final was.

'It still sounds like a game to me,' she said.

Talking to my wife was about as up-cheering as talking to our goalkeeper. I gave my eldest cub a cuff round the ear for breathing and then lay down in the corner of the cave to work out tactics. The only tactic I could think of was to pull a muscle on the morning of the match.

'I wouldn't have thought rabbits would be a problem,' said my wife later that night.

'That's because you haven't seen them play,' I said.

'Why don't you just eat them?' she suggested.

'Because,' I said witheringly, 'it's against the rules.'

'What rules?'

Once again I delivered a patient explanation.

'Hm', she said, when I'd finished, 'no problem.'

'What do you mean, no problem?' I asked.

'Leave it all to me,' she said.

'But you don't know anything about football!' I cried.

'Who needs to know about football?' she replied. 'You'll have your silly little cup, and then perhaps the rest of us can have some peace and quiet.'

Now, when my wife said she'd do something, she always did it, but how even she could turn a 50–0 defeat into victory was beyond my imagination. And then she told me her plan.

'You couldn't!' I said.

'I can,' she said. 'And I will.'

'It's not possible,' I said.

'You'll see,' she said.

The next day after breakfast – my wife didn't have any breakfast; she said she had to get into training right away – I took her along to the ground and showed her round.

'No problem,' she said again, 'so long as you're sure of the rules.'

'Sure I'm sure of the rules,' I said.

'In that case,' she said, 'the cup's yours.'

From that moment on, I had no doubts, but I didn't tell my team about the plan. Careless talk costs cups. I just laughed at their pessimism, astonished them with my confidence, and laid in a stock of goodies for our winners' party. They thought I was mad.

'Wolfie's gone goofy!' said Willy.

'50–0!' moaned Wilfie. 'And he's throwing a party!'

'Trust in your captain,' I said with the quiet authority of the born leader. 'The cup's as good as ours.'

At last the great day dawned. My wife was to make her own way to the ground, so I took the cubs and installed them on the terrace, where they had a vital part to play. Then I strolled into our changing room.

'50–0!' moaned Wilfie, our goalkeeper. 'I shall be the howling stock of the forest.'

'There's no point in our going out there,' said Willy, our striker. 'Let's strike.'

'Oh, ye of little faith!' I cried. 'I've told you we can't lose. Now, get ready to inspect the pitch.'

'Inspect the graveyard, more like it!' mumbled Wilfie.

Kick off was at 3 p.m. At 2 p.m. precisely, I led my team out to inspect the pitch. A loud cheer came from our supporters. These were my eight cubs – no other wolves had bothered to turn up. Who wants to see their team get beaten 50–0? From the millions of rabbits on the other side of the ground there were loud boos, which turned into cheers and a thumping of hind legs as the rabbit team came bounding on to the pitch.

'All ready for the slaughter, Wolfie?' mocked the rabbit captain.

'Ho ho, very funny, Bunny,' I said. 'But you'll soon be laughing on the other side of your bobtail.'

'Ha ha,' said Captain Rabbit. 'You must be the joker in the pack.'

'And I suppose you're the wit of the warren,' I replied, quick as a flash.

It was a clear verbal victory to me, even though he did slightly spoil it with some idiotic remark about me being the half-wit of the wolf-asylum. Then he led his team off one way, and I led mine off the other.

66

Before we disappeared into our changing room, I gave a secret signal to the cubs. At once they set up what I must confess was a rather unconvincing chant of 'We are the champions!' Unconvincing, but it did the trick. At once there was a storm of booing from the other side, and then a million rabbit voices began to sing their special football song 'You'll never walk alone.' It was an essential part of our plan. The louder they sang, the less they'd hear.

At 2.55 p.m. I led my team back on to the field. By now the ground was full – almost entirely of rabbits. With typical lack of sportsmanship they booed us all the way, but then they gradually fell silent as they waited for their heroes to come on to the pitch.

They had a long wait.

'Where are they?' growled Boris the Bear, who had been made referee because no one would argue with him.

'No idea,' I lied. 'Maybe they're scared of being beaten.'

All eyes were now turned towards the rabbits' changing room, but there was not a sound or a movement from there.

'If they don't hurry up,' said Boris, 'I shall award the match to The Wolves.'

'Oh, good heavens!' I said. 'What an absolutely dreadful idea!'

'Has anybody seen them?' bawled the bear, getting more and more sore-headed.

'Well, yes, we all have,' I replied. 'They were here half an hour ago, trying to frighten us off. Shall I go and see what they're doing?'

'Yes!' yelled the bear. 'And be quick about it!'

'Of course I will, sir,' I said, and trotted across the field.

I stopped outside the rabbits' door, and my voice rang out loud and clear through the hushed arena:

'Come along, my dears! The referee's waiting to start our game! We don't want to keep him waiting!'

There was no reply.

'Open the door!' roared Boris the Bear.

Obediently I opened the door.

'Well, fancy that!' I exclaimed. 'There's nobody here!'

A gasp of astonishment rabbited round the arena.

'There is absolutely nobody here!' I repeated. 'The little devils have run away. And they've even left the back door open!'

Indeed the changing room was completely empty. The only sign of our opponents was an odd ball of rabbit fur dotted around the floor.

'That's it!' roared Boris. 'No rabbits, no game. I award the cup to The Wolves.'

It was a proud day for me. Captain of the side that won the cup. My team mates carried me shoulder-high off the field. One or two spectators complained, of course, but since both teams had been on the field, and had been seen going back to their separate changing rooms, it was clear that no rules had been broken. No one could blame us if the rabbits had, so to speak, chickened out.

Our party went on all night and most of the next day. We had achieved the greatest upset in sporting history since the tortoise had beaten the hare. It was a pity my wife wasn't able to join in the celebrations, but I explained to my team that she didn't really like football very much. Besides, she was suffering from a bad attack of indigestion.

The Hyena that Wouldn't Laugh

Nina the hyena should have been rechristened Nona the moaner. She would sleep all day and moan all night and Henry, her husband, was fed up. Hyenas, after all, are famous for their laughter, but whenever Henry laughed, Nina would snap:

"A giggle never filled an empty stomach!"

Or: "You should be hunting, not hooting!"

Or: "You won't get a snack from a snigger!"

No one was allowed to enjoy themselves when Nina was around.

"Days are for sleeping," she would say, "and nights are for hunting. There's no room in the timetable for laughing."

Henry was a very mild hyena who didn't like trouble or hassle or fuss. He always allowed his wife first crack of the bone, always apologised to his prey before killing it, and always said thank you after eating it (though for some reason the dead animals never showed much appreciation for this courtesy). Above all, he liked to laugh, and he didn't see why he shouldn't laugh if he wanted to.

'If life's only for sleeping and eating,' he said to his brother Horace, 'one might as well be a hog as a hyena.'

'Ho ho ho!' laughed Horace, 'that's a good un!'

'Not bad, is it?' said Henry.

'What are you two laughing at?' snapped Nina. 'You won't get lunch from laughing!'

'Sorry, dearest,' said Henry. 'We didn't mean to upset you by enjoying ourselves.'

'I don't know why you married that crotchety creature!' said Horace to Henry when they were both out of earshot. And the two of them laughed so loudly that they came back into earshot.

'Stop your chortling and get on with your chasing!' shouted Nina.

'Certainly, darling,' called Henry. 'Anything you say, my precious.'

72

But although Henry bravely made light of his troubles, in truth he was not happy. He would wake up in the evening with a heavy heart, knowing that while there was a moon up above there would be a moan down below. If he didn't hunt, Nina would complain, and she would complain if he did. If he came home with a hare, she'd want a calf; if he caught a calf, she'd want a goat; if he got a goat, she'd want an antelope; if he loped in with an antelope, she'd want a stag; and if he staggered in with a stag ...

Well, one night he did stagger in with a stag. It was a real stroke of luck. A lion must have killed it and then abandoned it for some reason, and Henry let out a great whoop of "yum-yum" when he found it. For hyenas love stag-meat. Give stag-meat to a hyena, and it's like giving a banana to a monkey, fish to a cat, and chocolate fudge gateau to everybody you know. It needed Henry, Horace, and half a dozen helpers to drag this particular gateau back home.

'What's this?' snapped Nina when she saw them.

'It's a stag, dearest,' said Henry.

'I can see it's a stag,' said Nina. 'What's it doing here?'

'It's waiting to be eaten, sweetheart.'

'Well, I particularly wanted goat tonight.'

'I'm sorry, my beloved, but the takeaway were only doing stag.'

'That's very annoying,' grumbled Nina.

'Not getting her goat,' whispered Henry to Horace, 'has really got her goat!'

'Ha, ho, hi!' guffawed Horace.

'Guffaws never got a goat!' snapped Nina. 'Ah well, I suppose I shall have to make do with stag. Stand aside, then, and let me have a bite.'

But Henry did not stand aside. For Henry had had a rather remarkable idea. Despite his wife's moans, he knew that the stag was a once-in-a-lifetime discovery, and every hyena in the pack was wishing that he or she could have made it. So why not use it?

With a cry of 'Hi! Enas!' he summoned the whole pack to an emergency meeting.

'What are you up to now?' snapped Nina.

'Just trying to make you happy, oh light of my life,' replied Henry.

'Well, be quick about it,' growled Nina. 'I'm hungry.'

Henry's announcement was brief and to the point. There was to be a competition. The first hyena to make Nina laugh would win the prize. And the prize was the stag. 'Tell a gag, and win a stag!' cried Henry.

A howl of excitement rose from the assembly. There had never been a prize like this before, and surely it couldn't be *that* difficult to make a hyena do what comes hyenaturally. Soon they were all queuing up for the chance to bring a smile to the lips of a very unlaughing Nina.

The first competitor was Horace, who regarded himself as a specialist in funny faces. He crossed his eyes, swivelled his nose round to the right and his mouth to the left, waggled his ears, and stuck his tongue up his left nostril.

'At least it's better than your normal face,' snapped Nina, and Horace went away feeling rather stupid.

The second competitor was an acrobat. He stood on his nose, waggled his hind legs in the air, turned a somersault, crashed on to his belly, leapt high in the air, did a twist and a shake, and landed on one paw before falling flat on his face.

'Clumsy oaf!' snapped Nina.

The third competitor was a mimic. He put his front paws over his mouth and let out a woo-woo sound. Then he took his paws away and let out another woo-woo sound, which sounded exactly the same as the first. Then he stuck his hind paw in the air, twisted his neck up and round, and let out a third woo-woo sound which was identical to the first two.

'What's all that supposed to be?' snapped Nina.

'The first,' said the mimic, 'was an owl. The second was a dog. And the third was a wolf.'

'They all sounded to me like an idiot hyena,' said Nina and away went the third competitor.

The fourth was a comedian and he told Nina a funny story.

'This is a killer,' he said. 'Funniest story you've ever heard. A football match, right? Cup Final. Between the ants and the elephants.'

'I don't like football,' said Nina.

'It doesn't matter,' said the comedian. 'You'll laugh anyway. Ants versus elephants ... Cup Final ... great game ... nil nil, ten seconds to go, right? No score, ten seconds to go ... Little ant on the right wing ... '

'Ants don't have wings,' said Nina.

'Flying ants do,' said the comedian, 'ha ha ha ... how's that for wit?'

'Is that the end of the story?' asked Nina.

'No, no,' said the comedian. 'This ant comes flying down the right wing, see? Beats everybody, dribbles round the goalkeeper ... open goal ... just about to kick the ball into the empty net when, *scrunch*! The elephant goalie steps on him. Squashes him till he's simply non-exist-ant. And the crowd riots. The giraffe referee comes up to the elephant goalie, furious, note-book in hand, and he finds the goalie in tears. "What did you do that for!" asks the giraffe. "I'm sorry, I'm so sorry," sobs the elephant. "I didn't mean to squash him. I only wanted to trip him up." ' The comedian collapsed with laughter.

'Well?' asked Nina.

'Well, what?' howled the comedian.

'What's the joke?' asked Nina.

'He only wanted to trip him up!' screamed the comedian. 'Imagine an elephant tripping up an ant!'

All the hyenas were rolling around in hysterics – all except Nina.

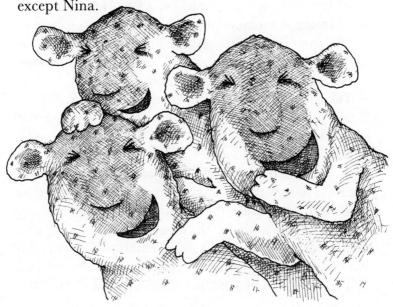

'Well, I don't like football anyway,' she snapped. 'Football is boring. And so was your story.'

So it went on. One hyena after another tried to make Nina laugh, but each one put her in a worse mood than ever, because now she was not just a misery – she was a hungry misery. She was hungry enough to eat a hare *and* a calf *and* a goat *and* an antelope. Or even a stag.

At last there was just one hyena left. He was an old, battle-scarred creature who could barely even hobble to the front of the crowd. As for his face, it was as mournful and moanful as that of Nina herself. It seemed to Henry that all hope was gone.

The ancient warrior limped right up to Nina and thrust his face very close to hers. Then he whispered something in her ear that no one else could hear. She looked at him. He looked at her. And suddenly the miracle happened. A smile came over Nina's face, and after the smile came a laugh, and it was as loud and as long and as look-on-the-bright-side a laugh as any hyena had ever added to the jangles of the jungle. Gasps of astonishment ran round the assembly, and Henry fell flat on his back and waved his paws in the air.

The old hyena heaved himself away towards the feast

that was his prize, while Nina laughed and laughed and laughed till it seemed her teeth would fall out. Henry bounded across to the prize-winner and got to him just before he reached his magnificent reward. And Nina was still laughing.

'The stag's yours,' said Henry. 'Congratulations. But tell me, please tell me, what did you say to my wife?'

'All I said was,' replied the old hyena, 'that if she laughed till I got as far as the stag, I'd give her half.'

Greasy Griff and Lady Antonia

Lady Antonia Ant was very busy. Lady Antonia Ant was always busy. Whatever the weather, the time of day, the direction of the wind, and the state of the nation, Lady Antonia Ant would be cleaning and clearing, toiling and tidying, hunting and heaving. Morning, noon and night, Lady Antonia Ant was busy.

Greasy Griff the grasshopper was always busy, too. He was busy leaping around, singing, eating, drinking, and generally enjoying himself. If there was a party going on anywhere, Greasy Griff would be in the thick of it, and if there wasn't a party going on, Greasy Griff would be trying to start one up. Morning, noon and night, Greasy Griff was having a good time.

'Whassamarrer wiv you, then?' he would say to Lady Antonia. 'Where's all this work getcher? Yer wanner enjoy yerself while yer can, like good ole me.'

'Just you wait till winter comes,' said Lady Antonia. 'Then you'll see where all this work gets me. And where enjoying yourself gets you.'

'I ain't scared o' winter,' said Griff, 'cos winter never comes.'

And off he went with a jolly jump and a cheerful chirrup, while Lady Antonia busily dragged a dead spider back to her store, mopped her brow, and went out to look for more dead spiders.

When autumn came, Griff's jumping was not quite so jolly, and his chirrups were a little less cheerful, but Lady Antonia simply went on cleaning, hunting and storing.

'You wanner gerrout an' enjoy yerself,' said Griff. 'Don't yer? I mean, life's short. Ennit? 'Ere terday an' gorn termorrer. Prob'ly.'

'Just you wait till winter comes,' said Lady Antonia. 'Then you'll wish you'd worked hard like me, instead of enjoying yourself.'

'Nah,' said Griff. 'Winter never comes. I 'ope.'

But of course winter did come. At first it was just a bit chilly, and Greasy Griff was still able to hop around and find himself enough food.

'Bit nippy terday,' he said to Lady Antonia. ' 'Ope it don't get nippier 'n this, or I'll be in trouble, eh, ha ha, huh!'

'It will,' said Lady Antonia. 'And you will.'

'Nah,' said Greasy Griff. 'I'll be orl right.'

But when the north wind started to blow, and the snow started to fall, Griff got very cold and very hungry, and so he made his way to Lady Antonia's residence and weakly knocked at the door.

'Who is it?' she called.

'It's m . . . m . . . me,' said Griff. 'Yer f . . . f . . . friendly neighbour'ood grass'opper, c . . . c . . . come ter cheer yer up.'

'I don't need cheering up, thank you,' said Lady Antonia.

'Well, I do,' said Griff. 'C . . . c . . . c'n I come in fer a bit?'

'A bit of what?' asked Lady Antonia.

'Well, a b . . . b . . . bit o' this an' a b . . . b . . . bit o' that would do nicely,' said Griff.

'Go and enjoy yourself,' said Lady Antonia.

'I w . . . w . . . would if I c . . . c . . . could,' said Griff. 'But I'm c . . . c . . . cold, so I c . . . c . . . can't.'

Lady Antonia was a kind-hearted ant, and so she opened the door and let the shivering grasshopper in.

'Not for long, though,' she said.

'Cor, it's nice an' warm in 'ere,' said Griff. 'Wish I 'ad a nice warm place like this.'

'A bit more work and a bit less whoopee,' said Lady Antonia, 'then you *could* have had a place like this.'

'An' look at all that food!' said Griff. 'Cor! You got enough food 'ere ter stock a supermarket!'

'A bit more labour and a bit less leisure,' said Lady

Antonia, 'and *you* could have had a food store like this.'

' 'S orl right fer you rich people, eh?' said Griff. 'Preachin' at us poor people. But it ain't fair. Why should you 'ave orl the warm an' orl the food while I ain't got none?'

'A bit more sweat and a bit less swagger,' said Lady Antonia, 'and you could have had as much warm and food as me.'

'That ain't my nature, though, is it?' said Griff. 'An' why should I be punished cos I've got a 'appy, cheerful, idle nature? It ain't my fault I don't like work.'

'Nor is it mine,' said Lady Antonia.

'I never said it was,' said Griff, 'but that don't make it no fairer, so this is what I'm proposin'. I'll stay 'ere wiv you right through the winter, an we'll go 'alves – 'alf fer you an' alf fer me. Now that's what I call fair.'

'It would have been fair if you'd done half the work,' said Lady Antonia, 'but since I did all the work, I don't see why you should get half the benefit, so I'll thank you to leave now.'

Lady Antonia pointed towards the door, beyond which the north wind howled loud enough to shiver the hairs on a grasshopper's leg. Griff announced that he wasn't leaving. Lady Antonia said he was. Griff said he wasn't. Lady Antonia said she'd bite him. Griff said he'd kick her. Lady Antonia said Griff was a big bounder. Griff said Lady Antonia was a little creep. Lady Antonia became indign-ant, and Griff became hopping mad. Lady Antonia said his behaviour was ant-isocial, and Griff said hers wasn't cricket. Lady Antonia said she found the whole business repugn-ant, and Griff said he was cicada whole thing.

Then Lady Antonia bit Griff in the left leg, and Griff kicked Lady Antonia with his right leg. This left Griff limping round the room saying "oh" "ah" and "ow", while Lady Antonia lay right in the middle of the room saying nothing.

'Oh! Ah! Ow!' cried Griff. 'I'll never chirrup again! Yer've ruined me fer life! Wot a way ter treat a friend! First yer try ter freeze me, then yer wanner starve me, an' now yer've gorn an' crippled me.'

And so he moaned and groaned and howled and hobbled until he found himself foot to face with Lady Antonia. He was about to give her another kick when he realized that she wasn't moving. Now no one had ever seen Lady Antonia motionless before, and the sight of her lying so still in the middle of the room suddenly took Greasy Griff's leg pains right out of his brain. And what came into his brain instead was the thought of a cosy little home with plenty of food to last him through the winter, protection against the cold, and no problems from complaining, leg-biting, grasshopper-hobble-making ants. If . . .

'Erm . . . are you orl right?' he asked. 'Can you 'ear me?'

Not a movement. Not a sound.

'You ain't . . . um . . . dead, are yer?'

Not a sound. Not a movement.

'Just say *yes* or *no*,' suggested Griff.

If Lady Antonia had said yes, Griff might have had even more of a problem than if she'd said no, but as it happened, she didn't say anything.

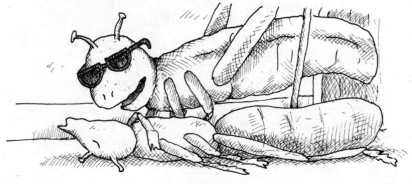

'You *are* dead, ain't yer?' said Griff, and very gently poked Lady Antonia with the tip of his toe.

He was right. She *was* dead. And Greasy Griff let out a chuckle and a chirp and a chirrup, as if high summer had come again.

'I dunnit!' he chortled. 'Got meself a 'ome, shelter an' grub, an' never done a stroke o' work. I'm brilliant! Wot a genius!'

And forgetting all about his injured leg, he leapt from one side of the room to the other in a dance worthy of a brilliant genius. And as he danced, he sang:

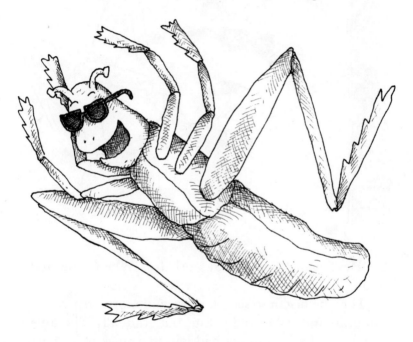

'Chortle chuckle, chirrup and chirp,
Only idiots go to work.
If you want a way of life that's brilli-ant,
Be like Griff an' go an' kill a silly ant.'

But he soon finished dancing and singing because he was now extremely hungry and, as Lady Antonia might have told him, dancing and singing couldn't fill an empty stomach. He hopped over the dead body of his hostess and made for the food store, smacking his lips in anticipation of the huge feast that was awaiting him. What he found was a collection of spiders, flies, bugs, beetles, bees, butterflies ...

'Hey!' said Griff. 'What's orl this? Where's the *real* food?'

Then he began to search more and more desperately for grass and leaves and plants, but gradually it became clear that Lady Antonia had laid in a stock of nothing but meat, and if there was one thing that Griff couldn't eat, it was meat ...

When Lady Antonia's brothers and sisters finally broke down the door, they found Lady Antonia and

Griff lying next to each other on the floor, both equally silent, equally motionless and equally dead. Lady Antonia was buried beneath a monum-ant, and Greasy Griff was placed in the p-antry. And to this day, ants still tell the story to little ants, while grasshoppers tell it to little grasshoppers. But they each end the story in a different way. The ants finish up by saying:

> "In winter if your door is knocked,
> Make sure that it stays firmly locked."

Whereas grasshoppers say:

> "If you are unfit to labour,
> Don't rely upon your neighbour."

The Hedgehog that Saw Winter

'Do as you're told!' said Mrs Hedgehog. 'We all have to go to sleep in winter.'

'Why?' asked little Harry Hedgehog.

'Because all hedgehogs go to sleep in winter,' said Mrs Hedgehog.

'Why?' asked Harry.

'Because hedgehogs have always gone to sleep in winter,' said Mrs Hedgehog.

'Why?' asked Harry.

'Don't keep saying *why*,' said Mrs Hedgehog.

'Why not?' asked Harry.

'Because I say so,' said Mrs Hedgehog. 'Now go to sleep.'

But Harry didn't want to go to sleep. Harry wanted to hunt worms and slugs, to play in the dead leaves, and to drink milk in the cowshed. *That* was what hedgehogs ought to do – not curl up into spiky balls and snore oompah oompah all through the winter, as his father, brothers and sisters were now doing.

'Your eyes are still open,' said Mrs Hedgehog.

'So are yours,' said Harry.

Thump!

'Ouch!' said Harry, as Mrs Hedgehog decided to stop speaking and to start spanking.

Harry closed his eyes. But closing the windows is not the same as putting out the lights. He would *not* go to sleep. He would stay awake, and so become the first hedgehog to see the winter. Mrs Hedgehog had said that the winter was dangerous, but if all hedgehogs went to sleep in winter, *how could she know?* Maybe winter was the most exciting time of the year, and hedgehogs missed all the fun just because mother hedgehogs felt sleepy.

It was not long before Harry heard the familiar kwee-kwah of his mother's snore, and with a kwee-kwah here and an oompah there he knew that his moment had come. He opened his eyes, uncurled himself, stood up, and tiptoed out into the winter world. He would now see what no hedgehog had ever seen before him.

What he saw was grey sky, bare trees, green grass and brown earth. In fact the winter world looked no different from the autumn world.

' 'Allo, 'Arry!' called Robbo the Robin from up in a chestnut tree. 'Wotcher doin' out at this time o' the year?'

'I thought I'd come and see the winter,' said Harry. 'But where is it?'

'It's on its way,' said Robbo.

'What will it do when it gets here?' asked Harry.

'What will it do?' echoed Robbo. 'It'll make an icehog out of you, 'Arry. You'll get a chill in the chest, a freeze in the knees, and a shiver in yer liver. I'd go back ter the nest if I was you.'

'It gets cold, does it?' asked Harry.

'Cold?' said Robbo. 'It's so cold, it puts pimples on yer pimples.'

'I haven't got pimples,' said Harry.

'You will 'ave,' said Robbo.

But Harry was determined to see the winter, and so he walked on. It *was* getting colder. There was a wind blowing now that seemed to stick spikes between his spikes, it was so sharp. He was also hungry, and so he was very pleased to come across an earthworm that was trying to work out which end of itself was which.

'I don't know,' said the worm. 'Am I going this way or that way?'

'You're coming my way!' cried Harry, and pounced on the worm.

'Ouch!' said the worm. 'You feel just like a hedgehog.' (Earthworms are blind, which is another reason why they never know which way they're going.)

'I am a hedgehog,' said Harry.

'Then what are you doing out at this time of the year?' asked the worm.

'I thought I'd come and see the winter,' said Harry.

'That's not fair!' said the worm. 'Oh, I'm so unlucky! Hedgehogs aren't supposed to catch worms in winter!'

'And what are *you* doing out?' asked Harry.

'That's also bad luck,' said the worm. 'I thought I was in.'

'Well, you are now,' said Harry, and gobbled the worm up, in and down.

He'd just finished swallowing the end of the worm (or was it the beginning?) when something cold and wet landed on his nose. At first he thought a bird might have done something rude on him from above, but

when he looked up, he saw a cloud of white flakes drifting down from the sky. Some of them fell on him and seemed to melt away, but others stayed on the ground and began to turn it white.

'What is it?' asked Harry.

'It's snow,' said Mr Squirrel from his nest up in the oak tree.

'What's snow?' asked Harry.

'What's snow?' repeated Mr Squirrel. 'Snow is ... well, you know how grass is grass?'

'Yes,' said Harry.

'And earth is earth?'

'Yes.'

'Well,' said Mr Squirrel. 'Snow is snow. That's what snow is.'

'Ah!' said Harry.

He jumped around for a while, catching snow flakes. First he caught one on his forehead, then he caught one on his nose, and then he put out his tongue and caught one on the end of that. It had a funny tingly taste. Then he stuck out his front foot and caught a flake, and he stuck out his back foot and caught another flake, and he stuck out his front *and* his back feet and fell flat on his tummy.

'This is fun!' he called out to Mr Squirrel. 'Why don't you come and play?'

'I'm too busy,' said Mr Squirrel.

'What are you doing?' asked Harry.

'Nothing,' said Mr Squirrel. 'And I'll never get to the end of it.'

Harry soon grew bored with catching flakes. After all, once you've caught a flake, there's nothing much you can do with it. And the same applies to the next flake. And the next. So he played a new game: he followed his own footprints. This was fun, too, until he found that he was simply going round in circles.

By now, the hills and fields and trees were all covered in white. It was as if a giant hand had tipped a giant jug of milk over the earth. The world in winter was as beautiful as a slither of slugs or a wiggle of worms.

But soon the flakes began to come down thicker and faster. The snow became difficult to walk in, and instead of footprints he was leaving legprints and then tummy prints. It wasn't fresh and tingly any more, but cold and wet, and rather than him catching the flakes, he had a horrible feeling that the flakes were catching him. Seeing the winter had been a good idea. But maybe not seeing the winter would have been a better idea.

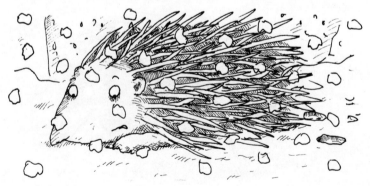

It was time to go home. Only how do you go home when you can't see and you can't move? Harry was lying on a white carpet, wrapped in a white blanket, and surrounded by a white curtain. Even if you had known he was there, you would never have seen him. And if you hadn't known he was there, you'd have thought nothing was there—except, of course, snow.

Harry curled himself up into a spiky ball and closed his eyes. If he couldn't see the winter, perhaps the winter wouldn't see him. In any case, he felt very tired—at least, those parts of his body that he could still feel felt tired. Those that he couldn't feel felt nothing at all. His last thoughts were of his mother who had told him winter was dangerous. She'd been wrong. Winter was deadly.

When the sun came out and melted the snow away, it revealed a small, spiky ball on the grass near the oak tree. Harry wasn't in it. Harry had gone to Valhoga, which is Heaven for hedgehogs.

'A waste of a good hedgehog, that was,' said Mr Squirrel looking down from his oak branch.

'Well, 'e wanted ter see the winter,' said Robbo the Robin, 'so 'e got what 'e wanted.'

'It's a pity, though,' said Mr Squirrel. 'Because now he'll never see the spring.'

The Flying Ostrich

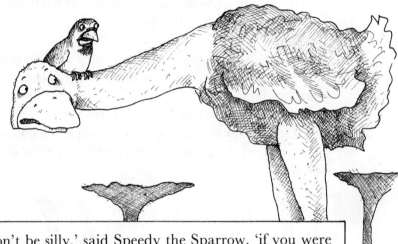

'Don't be silly,' said Speedy the Sparrow, 'if you were a bird, you'd be able to fly.'

'I *am* a bird' said Ozzie the Ostrich, 'and I've got wings to prove it.'

'What's the use of wings if you can't fly with them?' said Speedy.

'I *can* fly with them,' said Ozzie. 'At least, I think I can.'

'Fly?' cried Speedy. 'With a body like yours?'

'What's wrong with my body?' asked Ozzie.

'What's wrong with it?' repeated Speedy. 'What's right with it? Just look at it!'

Ozzie's neck performed a forward somersault, a backward somersault, a round O, a flat C, and a loop-the-loop.

'What are you doing?' asked Speedy.

'Looking at my body,' said Ozzie. 'And it's a very nice body.'

'It may seem nice to an ostrich,' said Speedy, 'but to a bird like me, it looks like a disaster. It's too big, it's too heavy and it's too droopy.'

'Droopy?'

'Droopy. Your feathers look as if they've been dipped in the river and hung on your body to dry. Then there's your legs.'

'What about my legs?' asked Ozzie.

'Pink tree trunks,' said Speedy. 'Even if you could get your body off the ground, you'd never get your legs to follow it.'

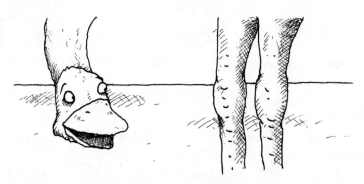

'I've got beautiful legs,' said Ozzie.

'Beauty,' said Speedy, 'is a matter of opinion, but flying is a matter of flight, and your legs are not a matter of flight. They're all right for standing, running, or lifting you up to look over fences, but when it comes to gliding through the air, legs like those are as much use as a pair of pink step ladders. Then there's your neck.'

'My neck?' echoed Ozzie.

'Your neck,' repeated Speedy.

'My neck's nice and long and stretchy,' said Ozzie.

'So is a piece of elastic,' said Speedy. 'But it won't help you to fly. Face the facts, Ozzie. With a body and legs and a neck like yours, you'll never be able to fly and so you cannot be a bird. Right?'

'Wrong!' said Ozzie. 'I *can* fly. Just you watch.'

Speedy perched on a branch and watched. Ozzie stood on tiptoe, flapped his wings, and jumped high in the air ... and came straight back down to earth.

'I'm just a little out of practice,' said Ozzie. 'Now then ... watch!'

Speedy watched. Ozzie stood on tiptoe again, flapped his wings again, and jumped high in the air again ... and came straight back down to earth again.

'Well, I did fly a little then,' he said.

'That,' said Speedy, 'is not called flying. It's called jumping.'

'I think I need to take a run,' said Ozzie.

'I think you need to take an aeroplane,' said Speedy.

'You just watch,' said Ozzie.

Speedy just watched. He saw Ozzie begin to run. The mighty pink tree-trunk legs whirled faster and faster, and the stretchy elastic neck stretched further and further, and the floppy wings flapped and waggled almost as fast as the legs whirled. But the feet still wouldn't leave the ground. He tried jumping as he ran. He must certainly have beaten the world high-jump record and may well have beaten the world long-jump record, but jump-stretch-flap-waggle as he would, he kept coming straight back to earth as if he were tied to it. And when he had run about four hundred metres (probably breaking the world record for that, too), he stopped for a puff and a blow.

In the distance he could see Speedy sitting on the branch, though Speedy didn't seem to be sitting very steadily. In fact he was rocking from side to side, twittering and holding his ribs.

Ozzie took a deep breath, drew his neck right back until his head was almost level with his tail, raised his right foot high in the air, shouted 'One, two, three, CHARGE!' and hurled himself into another high-jumping, long-jumping, stretching, flapping, waggling run towards Speedy's tree. Dust, plants and feathers flew, but Ozzie didn't. And Speedy was laughing so hard that he finally fell off his branch. (But, of course, being a bird, he simply joggled his wings and flew straight back on again.)

'It's no good,' puffed Ozzie. 'I just can't seem to get lift-off.'

'You're getting lift-off,' said Speedy, 'but you're not getting stay-off.'

'Why?' wailed Ozzie.

'Because,' said Speedy, 'you're not a bird. Now a bird simply flaps its wings, and hey oop ...'

Speedy jumped off the branch, flew three times round Ozzie's head, and landed back on the branch.

'You see,' he said, 'feathers light and straight, no neck stretching, legs tucked up ...'

'Swans fly,' said Ozzie.

'What about it?' asked Speedy.

'Swans have long necks. And herons fly.'

'What about it?'

'Well, herons have long legs. If swans and herons can fly, then why can't I?'

'Because,' said Speedy, 'you're not a bird.'

'I am,' said Ozzie. 'I am, I am, I am. I could fly if I just knew how to do it.'

'I could pick up an elephant,' said Speedy, 'if I knew how to do it. You can do anything if you know how to do it. That's a silly answer.'

'Just show me once more,' pleaded Ozzie. 'So I can watch you.'

Ozzie watched as Speedy jumped off the branch, flew three times round his head, and landed back on the branch.

'As easy as nibbling nuts,' said Speedy. '*If* you're a bird.'

'Aha!' said Ozzie. 'Aha, aho, ahum! I think I know what my problem is.'

'Your problem,' said Speedy, 'is that you're not a bird.'

'Oh no it isn't,' said Ozzie. 'My problem is that I'm not getting enough air under my wings. I saw what you did, and you did something that I haven't been able to do.'

'Yes,' said Speedy. 'Fly.'

'You jumped off the branch,' said Ozzie. 'That's how you got air under your wings. But since I'm a lot bigger than you, I'd need to jump off the top of the tree to get enough air under mine.'

'And how do you propose to get to the top of the tree?' asked Speedy. 'By carrier pigeon?'

'I can't get to the top of the tree,' said Ozzie, 'but I can get just as high.'

'This I must see,' said Speedy. 'But in any case, Ozzie, I don't have to jump off a tree – I can fly straight from the ground.'

'That,' said Ozzie, 'is because you're a spindly speck of a sparrow. You only need to jump over a blade of grass to get enough air. But when you're a supercolossal bird like me, you need a supercolossal jump. You'll see. When I have air under my wings, I'll fly ten times faster and further than you.'

105

'Well, how are you going to get as high as a tree?' asked Speedy.

'Follow me,' said Ozzie.

He then set off at a high-stepping trot across fields, through woods, up hills, down dales.

'Hold on, Ozzie!' called Speedy. 'I thought you were just going to climb a tree. I didn't know you were planning to emigrate. How much further is it?'

'Only a few miles,' said Ozzie.

'In that case,' said Speedy, 'I'll hitch a lift.'

He settled down on Ozzie's back, and together they went down dales, up hills, through woods, and across fields, until at last ...

'The sea!' cried Speedy.

They were standing at the top of a high cliff, and way below them, stretching out as far as the eye could see, was the shining blue ocean.

'Here we are,' said Ozzie. 'Now we'll see who can fly.'

'Wait a minute!' said Speedy. 'You're not thinking of jumping from here, are you?'

'Yes, I am,' said Ozzie. 'I'll get plenty of air under my wings from here and then you'll see what sort of a bird I am.'

'The sort of bird you'll be,' said Speedy, 'is a dead one. You can't do it, Ozzie. You'll be killed.'

'Oh no I shan't,' said Ozzie. 'Now get off my back. I don't want you weighing me down.'

Speedy jumped off Ozzie's back and flew to the very edge of the cliff so that he could look down at the jagged rocks and foaming sea far below.

'Ozzie,' he said, 'this really isn't a very good idea.'

'Yes, it is,' said Ozzie. 'Now, you just watch.'

He stood with his toes poking out into space, and his legs bent, ready for launching.

'Ozzie,' said Speedy, 'I wish you wouldn't do this . . .'

'Sh!' said Ozzie. 'I'm trying to concentrate.'

'Well, just concentrate on those jagged rocks down there,' pleaded Speedy. 'Think what nasty holes they're going to make in your beautiful legs and body!'

'Nonsense!' said Ozzie. 'Rocks can't fly.'

'Nor can you,' said Speedy.

'Yes, I can,' said Ozzie. 'You just watch.'

107

And so saying, he jumped off the cliff.

'There you are,' he cried, 'I'm flying!'

'No you're not,' said Speedy. 'You're falling.'

'You're right!' cried Ozzie. 'Oh, what a mistake! He-e-elp!'

Poor Ozzie. He flapped his wings, he whirled his legs, he stretched his neck, and he shouted 'He-e-elp!' but the only direction he went was down. His friend Speedy flew down with him, though he couldn't fly as fast as Ozzie fell.

'I wish I hadn't ...' cried Ozzie, but he never said what he wished he hadn't, because just as he said 'n't', he landed on the rocks. He hit them so hard that even the rocks said 'Ouch!' Speedy landed beside him, but poor Ozzie was now a Wozzie, and a very messy Wozzie, too.

Speedy looked at the bits and pieces of his friend, and sadly shook his head.

'I told you you weren't a bird,' he said.

It so happens that Speedy was wrong, and Ozzie was right, for Ozzie *was* a bird. Or at least he had been one. But being right didn't help him much, did it?

The Werewolf

(A story told by Wolfie)
Uncle Willy's Uncle Wally was a werewolf. Ugh, just thinking about it makes me go as shuddery as a sheep before dinner (*my* dinner, that is). Imagine living with a wolf that turned into a human being! The fright would kill you, even if he didn't.

The horrors began when he was just a cub. The family were woken one night by Winnie, one of the girl-cubs (my grandmother, actually). She was howling as if she'd lost a bag of lamb chops. In fact, according to her, she'd seen a human being in the cave.

'A human being?' growled Father Wolf. 'Don't be a ninny, Winnie. You were having a nightmare.'

'There was a human being here!' sobbed Winnie. 'It was horrible. It was standing on two legs, and was covered in pink skin!'

'It was just a bad dream, dear,' said Mother Wolf. 'There are no human beings here. Look for yourself.'

Everybody looked, and it was true – there was no sign of a human being. But Winnie also noticed that there was no sign of Uncle Wally.

'Wally's gone!' she screamed. 'The human being got him! The human being took Wally away!'

If the human being had been a bad dream, Wally's absence certainly wasn't. No one could have been more completely not there than Wally. The other cubs began to howl as loudly as Winnie, and the parents went rushing towards the mouth of the cave. But at that precise moment, in walked Wally.

'It's Wally! Where have you been? What happened? Did the human being take you away?' came a chorus of voices.

'Eh? What? Who?' said Wally. 'I only went out for a pee.'

Then, of course, everybody turned on poor Winnie, and it became a family joke: instead of going for a pee, everyone went for 'a human being'. Even Winnie began to think she'd simply had a nightmare.

Exactly a month later, a strange and terrible event occurred. The family awoke (all except Wally, who slept on and on) to find that one of the cubs was missing. It was little Wimpy, the smallest of them all.

'She's probably gone for a human being,' giggled a sister-cub.

'Or something even bigger,' sniggered a brother-cub.

But Wimpy didn't come back. And she didn't respond when the whole family joined in a Wimpy-where-are-you howl. And when they went outside to search, they found a clue that made them all feel as wobbly as a lamb's leg: in the soft ground at the entrance to the cave were the unmistakable footprints of a human being.

'I don't like the look of this,' said Father Wolf.

'And I don't like the smell of it,' said Mother Wolf.

'And we don't like the thought of it,' said all the little wolves, huddling together.

Wimpy was never found, and from that moment on, nobody felt like going to bed again. Nobody, that is, except Wally.

'Who's scared of human beings?' he would say. 'Human beings don't scare me. I could eat a human being for breakfast.'

'Mark my words,' said Father Wolf, 'with such courage, he'll be a hero one day.'

Indeed while all the other cubs fought to get to the back of the cave at night, Wally actually wanted to be at the front.

'Now that's sheer folly, Wally!' said Mother Wolf.

'Golly, Wally,' said his brothers and sisters, 'you'll be killed!'

'Call yourselves wolf cubs!' sneered Wally. 'You cubs have got as much courage as a leg of mutton in a ditch. The human being won't kill *me*!'

He was right, I guess. He had no reason to kill himself.

Two, three, four weeks went by, and nobody killed anybody. Maybe the monster had gone away; maybe Wimpy had fallen down a cliff; maybe the footprints belonged to a lost chimpanzee . . .

But then came the night of the full moon, exactly a month after Wimpy's disappearance, which had been exactly a month after Winnie's nightmare. This time it was Uncle Willy's father himself who saw the monster first.

'It was hideous!' he told Uncle Willy, many years later. 'Standing there on its hind legs, with its front legs hanging down by its sides. You could see its pink skin shining in the moonlight. Its face was smooth and flat – everything flat. Flat nose, flat mouth, flat teeth, flat ears – ugh, I've never seen anything so ugly in my life!'

The creature had been padding towards the cubs, stiff and upright, like a forked branch walking, when Uncle Willy's father had managed to unparalyse himself and let out a warning 'Yaaark!' Mother Wolf and three or four of the cubs woke up in time to see the pink monster rush out of the cave, and even Father Wolf, who was a very slow waker, said he'd glimpsed its hind leg.

'Wally's gone!' said Winnie, not for the first time. (Winnie was a Wally-watcher.)

It was true. Wally *had* gone. But that was peculiar, because they'd all seen the monster leave, and it hadn't taken Wally with it. So where was he? Mother Wolf wanted to search straight away. Father Wolf said it would be safer for the cubs if the search took place in daylight. Mother Wolf said Father Wolf meant it would be safer for Father Wolf if the search took place in daylight. Father Wolf said he knew what he meant, thank you very much, and he didn't need Mother Wolf to tell him what he meant, and the search would take place in daylight whatever he meant or whatever she said he meant.

The cubs were on Father Wolf's side, and so the search was put off till daylight. And when daylight came, so did Wally.

'Wally!' cried his mother. 'Where have you been? We were so worried about you!'

'Oh, I went for a human being,' said Wally.

'All night?' growled his father.

'I had a tummy upset,' said Wally.

'And a mummy upset,' said his mother. 'We thought the human being had got you.'

'What human being?' asked Wally. 'No human being could ever get me!'

'There's more to this than meets the muzzle,' growled Father Wolf.

But Wally was too exhausted to answer any more questions, and he settled down into a day-after-the-night-before sleep. Mother Wolf was worried about him because perhaps he wasn't well. Father Wolf was worried about him because perhaps he wasn't normal. The cubs were too worried about themselves to worry about Wally. But while he slept, Father Wolf went off to see Dr Lupus, the famous demanologist.

The news he brought back raised hairs where not even wolves know they've got them. Wally was a were-wolf: that's a wolf that turns into a human being whenever the moon is full. There's only one way to deal with a werewolf, and that's to kill him.

'But can't Dr Lupus cure him?' asked Mother Wolf.

'Only by killing him,' replied Father Wolf.

'I don't think much of that for a cure,' said Mother Wolf.

Mothers are like that. They always think their babies can do no wrong. I had a mother once. Boy, did I fool her! Anyway, Father Wolf explained to Mother Wolf that if they didn't kill the werewolf, he'd make the rest of the family into was-wolves.

'Either it's goodbye to him,' said Father Wolf, 'or it's goodbye to us. Personally I'd sooner say goodbye to him.'

'How are we going to kill him, Daddy?' asked Uncle Willy's father.

'There's only one way,' came the grim reply. 'You wait till the moon is full and he turns into a human being. And then ... ugh ... it's awful ... Then you ... ugh ... bite his bottom.'

A gasp of horror greeted this announcement, and no wonder. Can you think of anything more disgustingly ugh-ug-yuck than biting a human bottom?

'I'll bet it's poisonous,' said Uncle Willy's father.

'I'd die!' said Winnie. 'I'd just die!'

'It's going to need a lot of courage,' said Father Wolf. 'But a wolf has to do what a wolf has to do. I shall bite the blighter's bottom myself.'

Four weeks went by. Nothing special happened, except that nobody would play with Wally and only Mother Wolf would even talk to him.

'What's the matter with you guys?' he kept asking. 'What have I done? Is it my breath? Do I need a bath? Did I say something? Did I do something? What did I do? What did I say?'

Nobody told him.

And at last it was the bottom-biting night of the full moon. Father Wolf, licking his lips a little nervously, announced that he would be sleeping nearest the entrance.

'Why?' asked Wally. 'That's my place. I always sleep at the entrance. Why are you taking my place, Daddy? Daddy, why are you taking my place?'

'Hmmph,' grunted his father. 'Worple worple ...'

'I always sleep there, Daddy! Mummy, I always sleep there, don't I? It's *my* place, isn't it, Mummy?'

'Not tonight, dear. Not if Daddy wants to sleep there.'

'But why? Why, Daddy? Why, Mummy? It's my place! It's always been my ...'

'Shut up!' thundered Father Wolf. 'Or I'll ... I'll ... I'll bite your bottom off!'

A shudder passed all over Wally's body, and his eyes widened with fear. Then he sloped off into a corner, mumbling strange-sounding words that no ordinary wolf would know.

'Goodnight, everybody!' called Father Wolf.

'Goodnight, Daddy!' replied all the cubs but one.

Then everyone settled down and pretended to sleep. The eyes all closed, and there were one or two pretend-snores, followed by giggles, but soon the cubs fell very quiet. Each one could feel his own heart beating just a little bit faster.

Suddenly, from Wally's corner there was a strange sound of stretching and tearing. The closed eyes opened, and what they saw was the astonishing sight of Wally standing on his hind legs, with his skin slowly turning itself inside out. Within a minute, Wally the Wolf had changed into the hideous human monster we all fear.

Only one pair of eyes had failed to open. They belonged to Father Wolf, who was snoring loudly from the entrance to the cave. He was fast asleep.

Quietly the monster stalked towards him. It looked as if the family was about to become fatherless. But cometh the hour, cometh the cub. It was Uncle Willy's father himself who leapt from the ground, raced across the cave, and heroically sank his teeth into the monster's bottom. There was a cry of pain from the monster, and a cry of disgust from Uncle Willy's father, and the two of them fell groaning to the floor.

'Whassamarrer?' cried Father Wolf, startled out of his sleep.

'Ow! Ouch! Oo!' cried the monster.

'Ugh! Ugg! Yuck!' cried Uncle Willy's father.

'My poor Wally!' cried Mother Wolf.

'Hurray!' cried the cubs.

Suddenly every wolf fell silent, for there on the floor of the cave weird things were happening. The human monster was turning back into Wally! Little by little the sickly pink skin became covered with healthy wolf hair, the flat nose stretched out, the flat teeth pointed themselves, the flat ears began to taper, the close-together eyes slid round to the sides of the lengthening head . . . And there was the real Wally, dead but restored to wolfdom, as if he'd never been away.

It's a great story to tell at midnight, though Uncle Willy would tell it at any time. I did ask him why his Uncle Wally wasn't with us in Valhowla (Wolves' Paradise) so that we could all have a look at him, but he said werewolves weren't allowed here because they're too evil. That seems reasonable. I also said I'd like to meet his father – the hero that bit the werewolf's bottom, and had told Uncle Willy the story in the first place.

'Not possible, I'm afraid,' said Uncle Willy. 'He didn't make it to Valhowla, either.'

'Why not?' I asked.

'Because,' said Uncle Willy, 'all his life he was such a terrible liar.'

121

The End

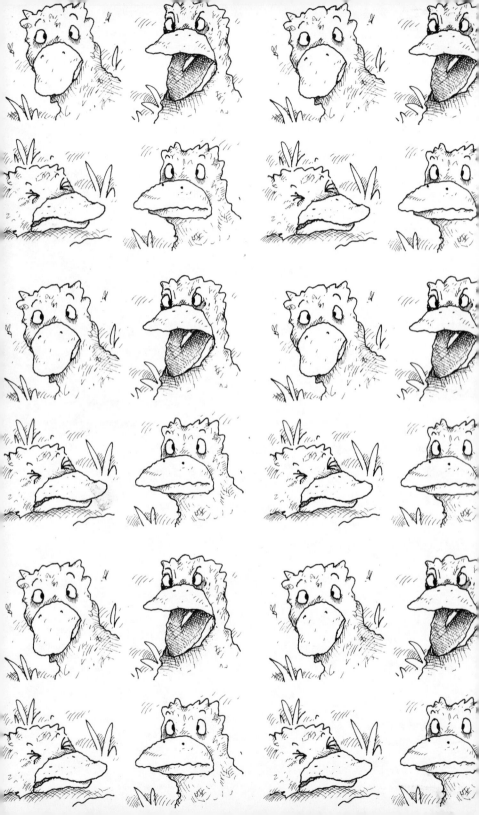